The Rugrats' First Kwanzaa

Based on the TV series *Rugrats*® created by Arlene Klasky, Gabor Csupo, and
Paul Germain as seen on Nickelodeon®

ISBN 0-439-36613-5

12 11 10 9 8 7 6 5 4 3 2 1   1 2 3 4 5 6/0

Printed in the U.S.A.

First Scholastic printing, November 2001

The Rugrats' First Kwanzaa

adapted by Stephanie Greene
from the script by Lisa D. Hall, Jill Gorey, and Barbara Herndon
illustrated by Segundo Garcia

SCHOLASTIC INC.

New York Toronto London Auckland Sydney
Mexico City New Delhi Hong Kong Buenos Aires

It was the day after Christmas and a storm was howling outside. Susie had invited her friends over to play with her special Christmas present.

"Ooh, Chuckie, your hairs is so cute," said Lil. "You look like a porkypine!"

"Do me next, Susie," said Kimi. "I want to look like a porkypine too!"

Just then a fierce gust of wind blew the door wide open. It was Susie's Aunt T!

"Ooo-hoo-hooey! I haven't seen a storm like this since Hurricane Coco in Tahiti!" she shouted.

"It's so good to see you, Aunt T!" Susie's mom said. "Where's Uncle Charles?"

"In Zanzibar, the old goat," Aunt T chuckled. "Not to worry, he'll catch the next flight out."

"Come here and give your Aunt T a big hug, children. I have a feeling we're gonna have an extra special Kwanzaa this year."

"What's Kwonzo?" Susie asked shyly.

"Kwanzaa commemorates the first harvest celebrations of Africa," said Edwin.

"Sugar," Aunt T told Susie, "all you have to know is that Kwanzaa is about being together as a family to honor our great people!"

After Aunt T finished decorating she started beating on a drum.
"Let the music move you, little ones!" she shouted.
Move us where? wondered Tommy, as he leaped and spun and shook his hands in the air.

Aunt T spun to a stop in front of the fireplace. "Look at all these awards!" she marveled.
"A lot of special people live here," Randy said proudly.
"Let's have the *karamu*, the big feast, tonight to celebrate," Aunt T said.

"Which one of those 'wards is yours, Susie?" Kimi whispered.
"None of 'em," Susie said sadly. "I guess I'm not special like everybody else."
Kimi put her arm around Susie's shoulder. "Well, I think you're great."

Aunt T reached into her suitcase and fished out a large pouch. "*Habari gani!*" she said. "That's Swahili for 'How are you?' You're supposed to answer '*Umoja.*' That means 'Unity'— everyone together on the first day of Kwanzaa."

"Uh, *Umoja,* Aunt T," they said.

Aunt T tossed each of them a present. "You share this with your little friends," she said, handing the last one to Susie.

"C'mon, Susie," Tommy said excitedly. "Open your Kwonzo present!" Susie ripped the paper off.

"It's nice," Chuckie said politely. "But what is it, eggsackly?"

"Just a dusty, old book with some pictures in it," sighed Susie.

Tommy looked at the other presents. "Wow! Look at the neat stuffs *they* got!"

"All right, Carmichaels, time to get ready for our Kwanzaa feast!" Aunt T bellowed. "Buster, you help with dinner. My recipe for African peanut-butter stew will knock your socks off! Alisa, you can set the table. Don't forget the *Muhindi*, the *Mkeka*, and the *Mazao*."

Alisa looked confused. "Excuse me?"

"That's corn, straw mats, and fruits of the harvest," Edwin explained.

"Edwin, you get the *kinara*—that's the candle holder," said Aunt T. "Let's get cracking!"

"But what about me, Aunt T?" Susie said. "I want to help with Kwanzaa too!"

"We can help you get the candles for the 'nara, Susie," said Kimi, pointing to the mantle.

"How we gonna get way up there?" asked Chuckie nervously.

"We can make a ladder outta peoples!" said Tommy.

The babies piled on top of each other to form a pyramid. Susie climbed on top.

"Quit wigglin', Chuckie," said Phil.

"I can't help it," said Chuckie. "My big-boy pants are creepin' up on me."

CRASH! The pyramid came tumbling down.

Susie sighed. "I'm not good at anything," she said sadly.

"Maybe you could be an imbentor like Edwin," said Phil.

"Yeah," said Kimi, "and imbent a cure for being 'fraid of the dark."

"Or be a prezdent of somethin' like Alisa," suggested Lil.

Phil scratched his head. "What's a prezdent do again?"

"They talk a lot," said Lil, "and smile when they get their pictures taked."

"I don't want to do somethin' *they're* good at," Susie said. "I want to do somethin' *I'm* good at."

"You're good at makin' stuffs," Chuckie said.

"That's it!" Susie said. "I'll make Aunt T a Kwanzaa present!"

"Gee, that's a real nice lumpy ball, Susie," Chuckie said.

"Actually it's a sculpture of Aunt T," Susie said.

Phil was tugging at the headdress Lil was wearing. "It's my turn to wear the feathers!"

"Nuh-uh, Philip," said Lil, tugging back. "You already got to be the chicken!"

"Watch out!" warned Susie.

Plop! The sculpture fell to the ground.

Susie grabbed the sculpture and ran to her room.

Aunt T heard the racket and went up after her. "What happened, baby?" she asked.

"The present I made for you got ruined," Susie sniffed. "I guess you're gonna hafta celebrate Kwanzaa without me."

"Bless your heart, child," said Aunt T, looking at the sculpture. "It's not perfect, but it's got a lot of character. Just like me!"

"But, Aunt T, I can't celebrate Kwanzaa 'cause I'm not great," Susie said. "I don't have any trophies or 'wards like the rest of my family."

"Baby, greatness doesn't come from winning awards," Aunt T said.

"It doesn't?" asked Susie.

"No, ma'am. Greatness is inside." Aunt T stood up. "Come on. I've got some people I'd like you to meet."

"It may not look like it, Susie, but the present I gave you is very special," Aunt T said. "I've kept this scrapbook for nearly fifty years. It's filled with all sorts of great people."

"I bet she's gonna tell us a Kwonzo story!" whispered Phil.

"Ooh, I haven't heared a Kwonzo story since . . ." Lil thought for a second, "since ever!"

Susie pointed to a photograph in the scrapbook. "Who's that?"

"That's your Uncle Charles," said Aunt T. "Now, *he's* a great man. Helps anyone who needs it. And one day back in 1963, a very special gentleman needed help."

"That's us," Aunt T said. "Lookin' fine, and on our way to see Dr. Martin Luther King."

"Woo-wee!" said Edwin. "You mean in person?"

"Yep, except we didn't make it on time," Aunt T said. "There was a car in trouble on the road, and Charles stopped to help."

"Oh, no!" said Susie. "You didn't get to see the king?"

"Not in Washington, D.C. we didn't." Aunt T pointed to another picture.

"That's Uncle Charles, helping the stranger find out what was wrong with his car," said Aunt T. "You'll never guess who he was."

"Wow! That's Dr. Martin Luther King!" exclaimed Edwin. "Way to go, Uncle Charles!"
"But where's his crown?" asked Susie.

"Dr. Martin Luther King wasn't *that* kind of king," Aunt T said. "He was a humble man who taught people how to get along better, and became one of the greatest men in the history of our country."

"Uncle Charles never told me that story," said Randy, grinning proudly.

"This is fun!" said Susie. "Tell us more Kwanzaa stories!"

Aunt T turned the page, and Susie pointed to another picture. "Look! There's me!"

"That's not you, it's Mom," said Alisa. She peered at the picture. "Isn't it, Aunt T?"

"Sure is," said Aunt T. "On the day she sang her first solo in church. She was only six years old. It's one of the great moments in our family history."

"Mama looks so scared, I bet she couldn't even sing," said Susie. "Right, Aunt T?"

"Wrong," Aunt T said. "She was scared, all right, but she didn't let her fear stop her from doing what she loved."

"But what did she do?" asked Susie.

"She went out there and brought the house down, that's what!" Aunt T said.

"Oooh, child, my feet hurt, I danced so much that day!" Aunt T said.

"You know, I wasn't half bad," said Lucy, blushing.

"Great people get scared like everybody else," said Aunt T. "They just don't let it stop them."

"You're forgetting one of the greatest people of all, Aunt T," Lucy said. "One who brought her family together to share special memories during Kwanzaa."

"Who's that?" Aunt T smiled.

Susie pointed straight at her.

"YOU!"

"Always be proud of who you are and where you come from, Susie," Aunt T said. "And remember, you have your whole life to discover how great you really are."

She held out her hand. "Now, come on, let's go celebrate. I'll light the first candle on the *kinara* and you can give the unity toast."

"Those were the bestest Kwonzo stories I ever heared, Lillian," said Phil.
"Those were the onliest Kwonzo stories you ever heared, Philip," whispered Lil.
"Susie sure gots a great fambly," said Kimi.
"Yeah, and she's the greatest of 'em all!" said Chuckie.

Uncle Charles arrived just as the family was sitting down to dinner.
"Oh, Charles, you made it!" said Aunt T, jumping up to give him a big hug.
Lucy looked around the table. "It's been a wonderful day," she said. "I want to thank Aunt T and Uncle Charles for bringing our family and friends together."

Susie raised her cup of milk up high. "Thanks for showin' me we can all be great, Aunt T!"

"*Umoja!*" shouted Aunt T.

"*UMOJA!*" everyone called back.

What is Kwanzaa?

Kwanzaa is a seven-day holiday that takes place during the last week in December. It is a celebration of African heritage. More than twenty million people observe Kwanzaa in the United States, Canada, England, the Caribbean, and Africa.

During Kwanzaa, family and friends come together to remember the ancient African harvest ritual. The word Kwanzaa means "first fruits" in Swahili, and food is a big part of the celebration. Gifts are also exchanged, and children often receive three traditional gifts—a book that teaches something, a symbol of the past, and a simple toy.

The seven items central to the celebration of Kwanzaa are:

- **straw place mats**—*mkeka* (em-KAY-kah)
- **a holder for seven candles**—*kinara* (ki-NA-rah)
- **an ear of corn**—*muhindi* (moo-HIN-dee)
- **communal cup**—*Kikombe cha umoja* (kee-KOM-be chah oo-MO-jah)
- **a variety of fruit**—*mazao* (ma-ZAH-o)
- **modest gifts**—*zawadi* (zah-WAH-dee)
- **the candles**—*mishumaa* (mee-SHOE-mah)

On the first day of Kwanzaa it is customary to say *"Umoja,"* which means "Unity." One candle is lit on each night of Kwanzaa. There are three red candles to remember the struggle of African Americans, three green candles for hopes and dreams, and one black candle for pride.

After each candle is lit family and friends drink from the unity cup and toast their ancestors by saying *"Harambee!"* which means "Let's all pull together!"